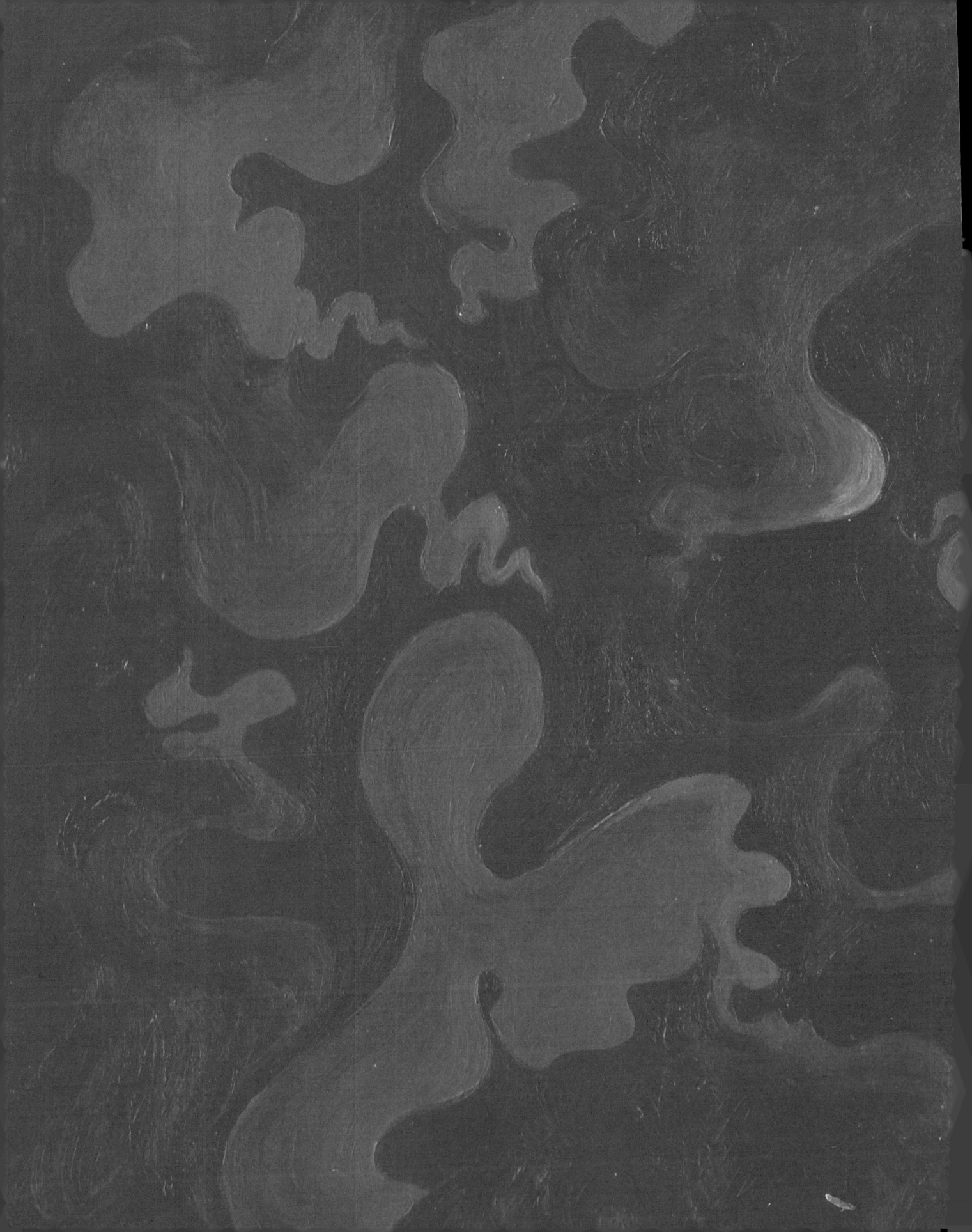

For Madison, Meadow, Makenzie, and every hair on their beautiful heads.

For girls with messy hair that will not be tamed.

-P. P.

Girl Problems: It's a Hairy Situation

By

Portia K. Phillips

Illustrated by La'Toya M. Smith

I woke up this morning, and I could not see my face.

This is a Girl Problem, I have curls all over the place.

It's so,

Big, and

Deep, and

SCARY

It's got a mind of it's own.

No matter what I do with it, it won't leave me alone.

Natural,  Curly, 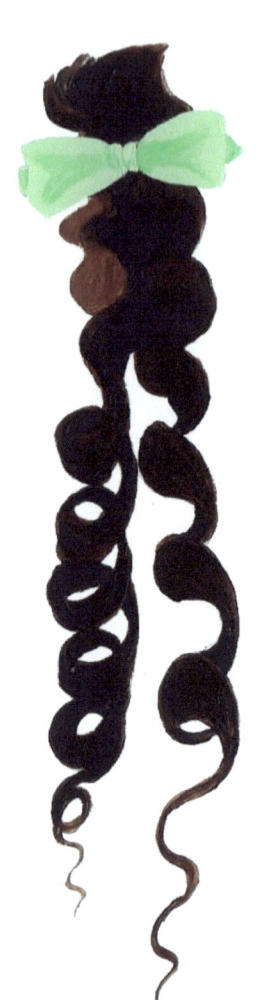 Kinky,

my hair has lots of names.

But when you

wet it, wash it,

or dry it,

it always stays the same.

They braid it, wrap
it, and twist it,

this hair won't stay
in place.

I'll comb it,
rub it,
and brush it,
but it's right
back in my face.

No matter how **sleek** I make it, it always starts to creep.

This hair of
mine I tell you,
I can never get
to sleep.

The one thing I can tell you is, I always look good.

I guess what I should be saying,
is my hair's misunderstood.

On hot days I strut proudly. I like it **bold** and **big**.

I can work so many looks, it's like I'm wearing wigs.

I said I have

Girl Problems,

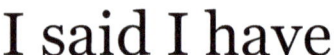

oh this I say

is true.

I know that

you will

under-

stand, be-

cause

I'm sure

that you do

too.

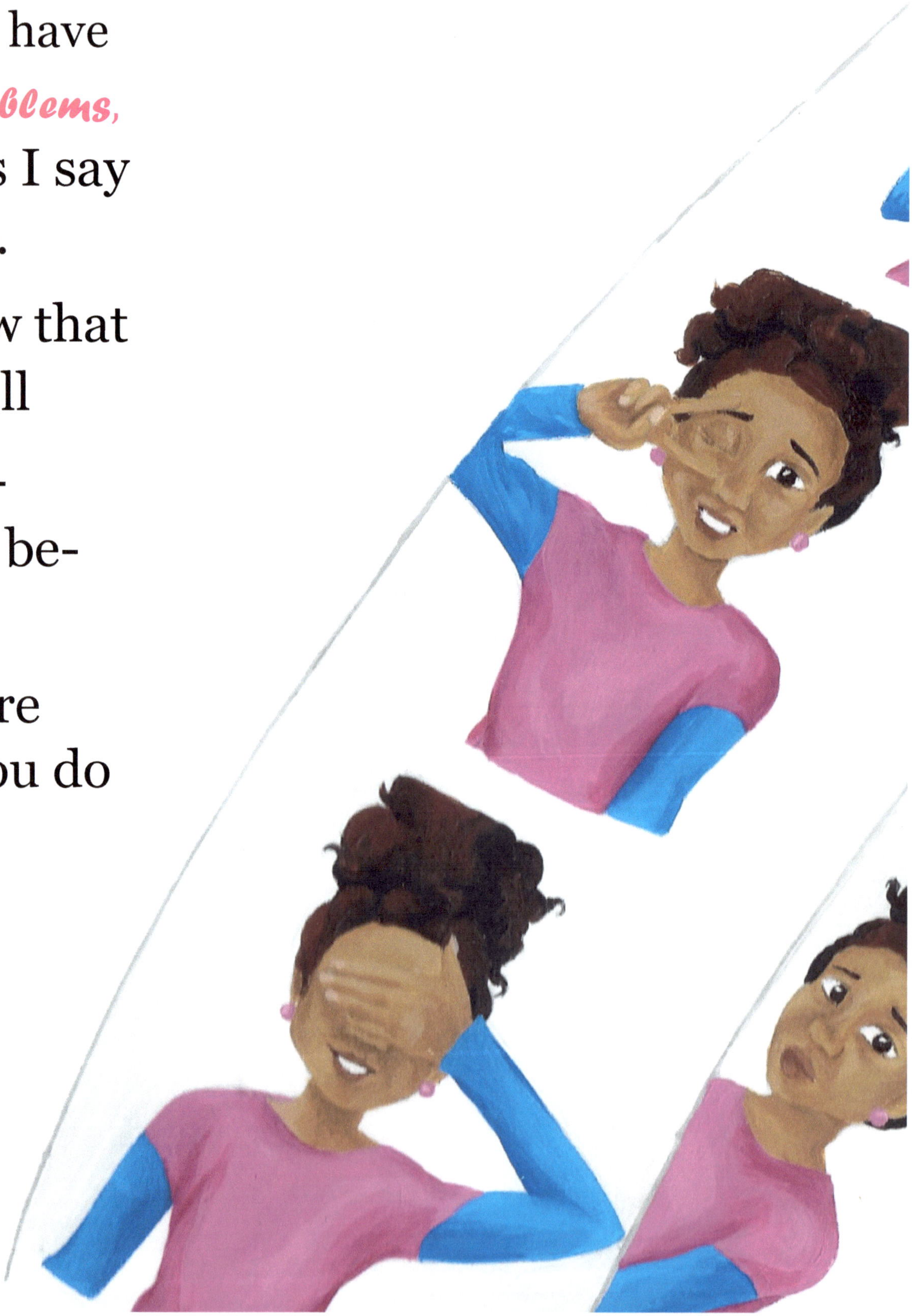

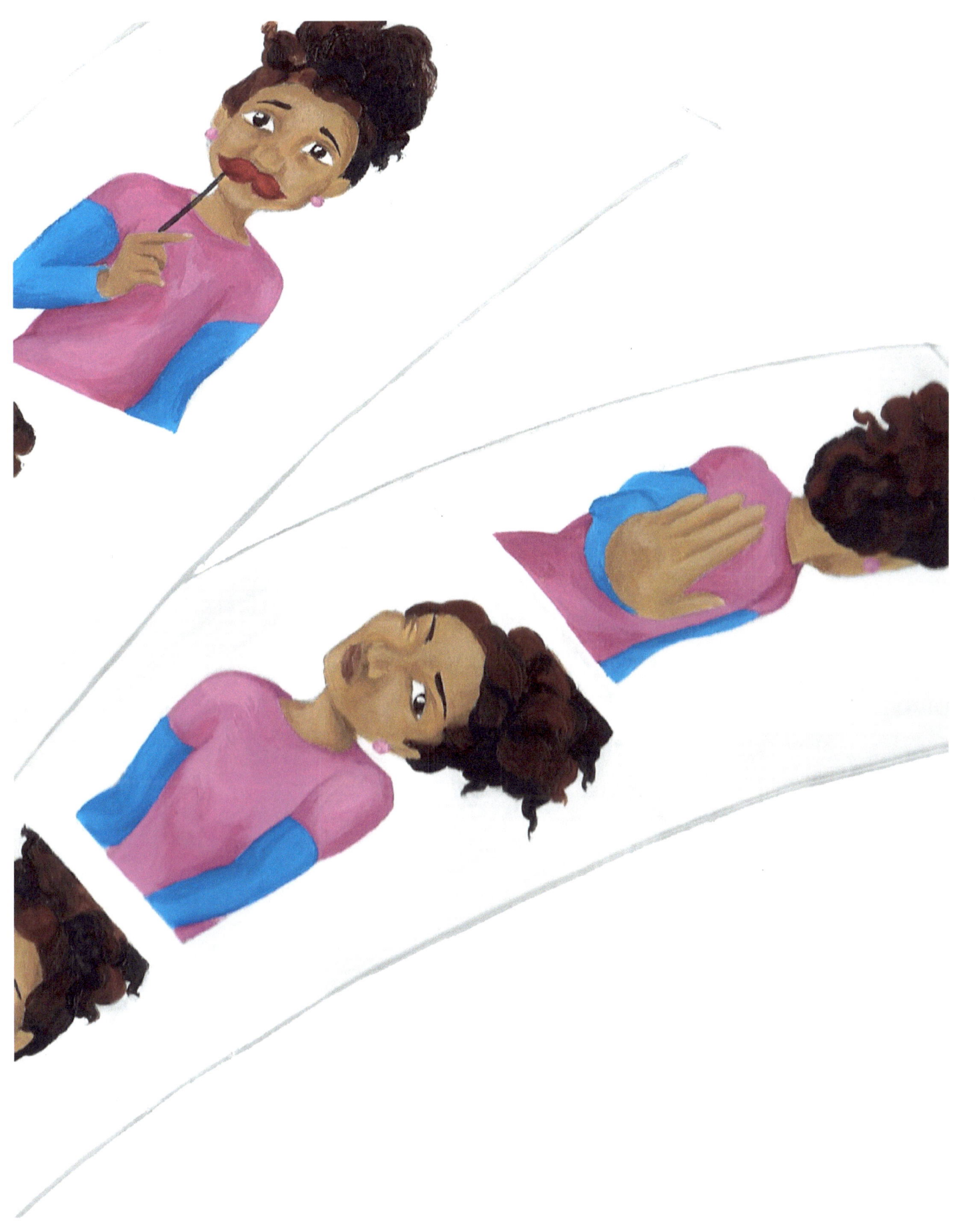

I hug and kiss these curls of mine,
because they're my *signature* look.

What will your *signature* look be, when you close this book?

My Inspiration

About the Author

Portia Phillips

Portia Phillips is a wife, mother, educator, who is adding author to her list of titles. As an educator she has had the opportunity to connect with children of all ages and backgrounds through literacy and believes that books help children to navigate their unique social lives. As a mom she has had the opportunity to view the world from her children's perspective and it inspired her to share their truth with other girls who may connect to it. Portia lives with her family in Texas and many more titles on the horizon that communicate the delightful views of young girls.

www.ingramcontent.com/pod-product-compliance
Lightning Source LLC
Chambersburg PA
CBHW041558120626
46551CB00002B/249